SLOATHAR
THE SLOTH

Written by
Paul Toms

Illustrated by
Novel Varius

Every three minutes a child is born with a
cleft lip and/or cleft palate.
This book is dedicated to all of you.

Published in association with
Bear With Us Productions

© 2024 Paul Toms
Sloathar the Sloth

ISBN: 978-1-3999-7132-4

Cover by Richie Evans
Design by Tommaso Pigliapochi
Illustrated by Novel Varius

www.justbearwithus.com

SLOATHAR THE SLOTH

Written by
Paul Toms

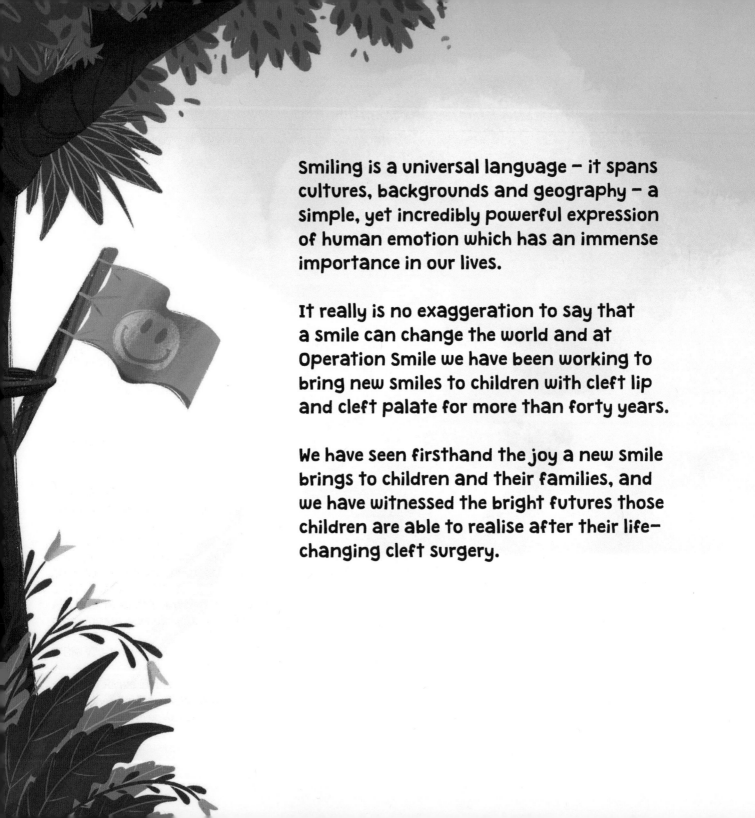

Smiling is a universal language – it spans cultures, backgrounds and geography – a simple, yet incredibly powerful expression of human emotion which has an immense importance in our lives.

It really is no exaggeration to say that a smile can change the world and at Operation Smile we have been working to bring new smiles to children with cleft lip and cleft palate for more than forty years.

We have seen firsthand the joy a new smile brings to children and their families, and we have witnessed the bright futures those children are able to realise after their life-changing cleft surgery.

I am therefore very grateful to Paul for his passion and commitment to supporting Operation Smile and for positively drawing on his own experience of having a cleft condition, and using it as his driver to help others.

It brings me joy to know this book will bring happiness to those families who read it together, as well as helping to fund more new smiles for children with cleft conditions.

Thank you sincerely to Paul, but also to you, for helping us spread new smiles to thousands more children around the world.

Kathy Magee, B.S.N., M.S.W., M.ED.
Co-Founder, President & CEO
Operation Smile

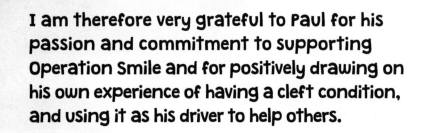

Sloathar's had a long hard day.
He's dreaming of his favourite food.
**Shhh! Shhh! Quiet please,
we don't want to wake him!**

All of a sudden, such a hullabaloo!
Sloathar's smile is turned upside down.
He's not asleep now!

"I'm a sloth and I just want to loaf," he grumbles.
What is that noise that has woken Sloathar up?
Let's go with him to take a look.

Moving as fast as a sloth can go...
"Which isn't very fast, you know!"
Curious Sloathar slides down his tree.

The racket is getting louder.
It seems to be coming from over there.
Is it something fierce and furry?

Sloathar wasn't expecting that!
"Oh, my word, this is quite absurd!
A beetle and her toys making so much noise!"

"I'll take those drumsticks.
One... Two... Thank you!"
Sloathar slowly loafs back to his bed.

He can sleep and smile again now.
Or can he?

"Now to dream of chocolate ice cream!"
Slowly his frown turns upside down.
Sloathar settles back to sleep.

"I'm a sloth and I just want to loaf," he mutters.
What is that noise that has woken Sloathar up?
Let's go with him to take a look.

Moving as fast as a sloth can go...

"I'm not as fast as you, you know!"
Grumpy Sloathar flumps down his tree.

The racket is even louder now.
It's coming from over there.
Is it something sharp and snappy?

BANG!

BANG!

BANG!

Sloathar wasn't expecting that!
"Oh, my word, this is quite absurd!"
The beetle is back, this time with a friend.

"I'll take those drumsticks. One... Two... Three... Four.
You won't be making a noise anymore!"
Sloathar bumbles back to his bed.
He can sleep and smile again now.
Or can he?

"Take a break to dream of cake!"
Slowly his frown turns upside down.
Sloathar slips back into a lovely sleep.

Moving as fast as a sloth can go...
"Faster than a snail, you know!"
Tired Sloathar trundles down his tree.

The racket is even louder now.
It seems to be coming from over there.
Is it something cheeky and cheerful?

Sloathar wasn't expecting that!
"Oh, my word, this
is quite absurd!"
The beetle is back, this time
with two friends!

"I'll take those drumsticks. Two... Four... Six.
Now the problem is fixed."
Sloathar lazily ambles back to bed.
But wait... What's this?

"Why the mood, dude?" the beetle asks.
She's noticed Sloathar isn't smiling.
**"That's not the style
on the Isle of Smiles!"**
she shouts.

"Well, it's the banging of the drums, you see.
It keeps me awake, up there in my tree.
What can be done, yet still be fun?"

SHHHH...

The beetle and her friends stop drumming.
"Turn Sloathar's frown upside down," they whisper.
"Whilst he's asleep, we won't make a peep!"

Sloathar wasn't expecting this!
"Oh, my word, not a sound to be heard!"
He can sleep and smile again now.
Or can he?

Water splashes on Sloathar's face.
"I'm a sloth and I just want to loaf!" Sloathar shouts angrily.
"I've been woken again, this time by the rain!"

Hold on one second.
All is not as it seems.
It's not rain trickling down through the leaves.

One... Two... Three...
"Oh, my word, what's this I see?
The beetles have no fun in the tree,"
Sloathar says sadly.

"Get off your bums and pick up your drums!"
Sloathar shouts. Playing together is much more fun.

"Two... Four... Six... Eight...

This beat is great!"
everyone sings.

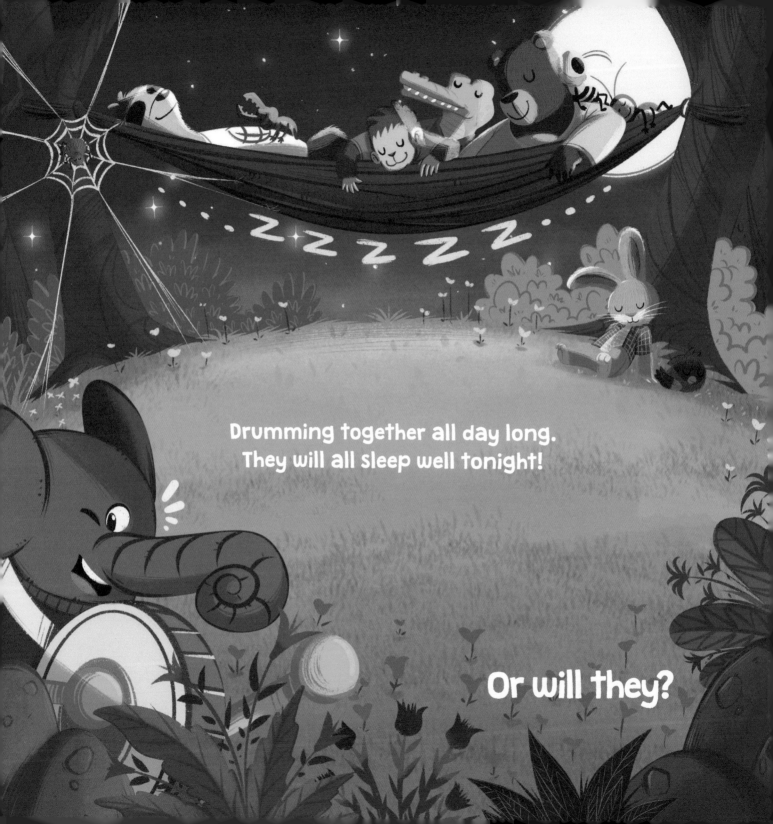

Drumming together all day long.
They will all sleep well tonight!

Or will they?

Printed in Great Britain
by Amazon

42467614R00021